WINTER
SLEEP

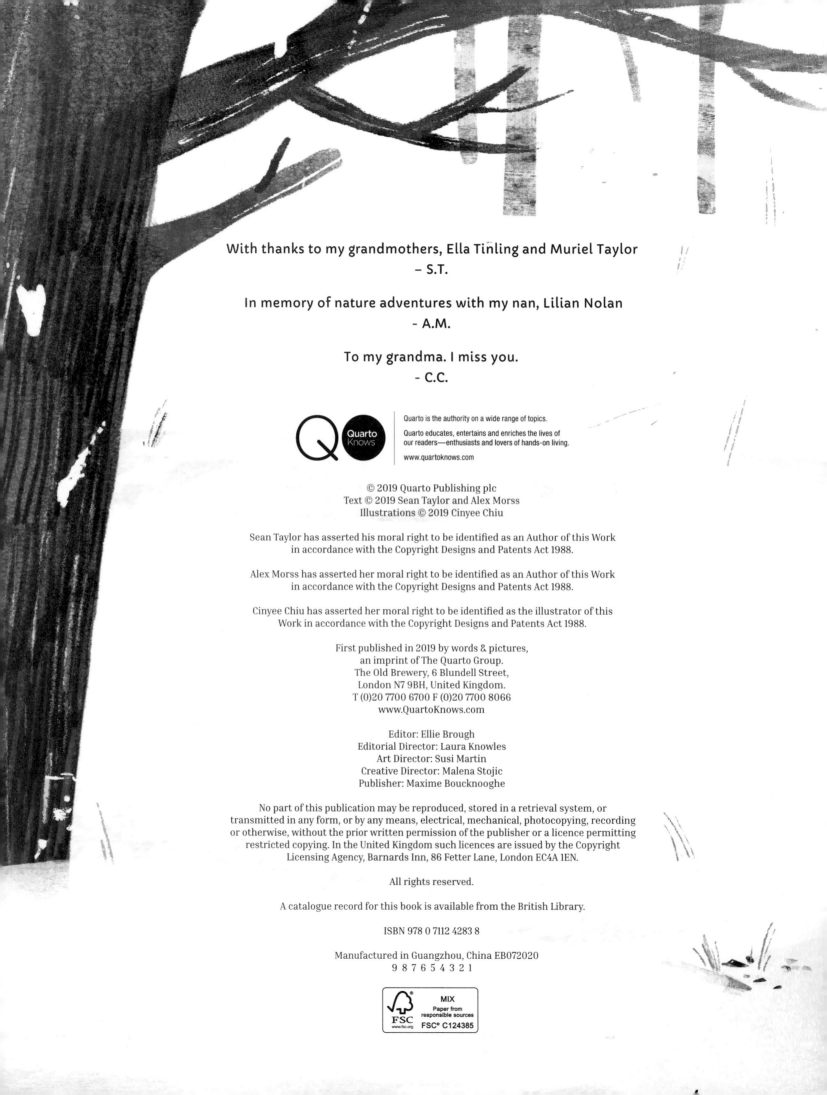

With thanks to my grandmothers, Ella Tinling and Muriel Taylor
– S.T.

In memory of nature adventures with my nan, Lilian Nolan
- A.M.

To my grandma. I miss you.
- C.C.

Quarto is the authority on a wide range of topics.

Quarto educates, entertains and enriches the lives of our readers—enthusiasts and lovers of hands-on living.

www.quartoknows.com

First published in 2019 by words & pictures,
an imprint of The Quarto Group.
The Old Brewery, 6 Blundell Street,
London N7 9BH, United Kingdom.
T (0)20 7700 6700 F (0)20 7700 8066
www.QuartoKnows.com

Editor: Ellie Brough
Editorial Director: Laura Knowles
Art Director: Susi Martin
Creative Director: Malena Stojic
Publisher: Maxime Boucknooghe

A catalogue record for this book is available from the British Library.

ISBN 978 0 7112 4283 8

Manufactured in Guangzhou, China EB072020
9 8 7 6 5 4 3 2 1

FSC
www.fsc.org
MIX
Paper from responsible sources
FSC® C124385

WINTER SLEEP

A HIBERNATION STORY

Sean Taylor & Alex Morss
Illustrated by Cinyee Chiu

words & pictures

When it was summer, I stayed at Granny
Sylvie's house. She knows lots of things.

Like the names of flowers
and how to spot a deer's hoof print.

And where to splash round the pond,

climb a slope of green ferns,

pass through oak trees
with moss on one side,

and find...

...the secret glade.

Butterflies fluttered, even though it was late.

Granny Sylvie helped me listen for songs of different birds.

It was still warm. We stayed right into the summer magic of the night.

And we kept so still, we saw the dormouse who lives there run up a hazel tree.

When I went back to stay with Granny,
it was winter.

I asked her, "Can we go to the secret glade?"

She said, "Yes. If you can find it!"

Everything was different.
The pond was frozen hard.
The ferns on the slope looked dead.
The oak trees with moss on one side
were all bony.

And the glade was quiet and bare.
It wasn't anything the same.
No butterflies. No flowers. No birds.

I wanted to see the dormouse. But Granny said,
"The dormouse will be having a winter sleep."

It was too cold to stay.
And I said, "Nothing's *alive* in winter!"

Granny Sylvie told me, "It is…"

"We can't see the dormouse, but she's hiding here. She'll be safely, deeply sleeping, all winter long. This is her hibernation time.

In autumn, she feasted on forest nuts, fruits and insects. Then the long nights came. She felt cold, heavy and sleepy. There was nothing more to eat.

So she made a nest ball. And she's inside, secretly snoring until the spring sun warms her body again."

On the way back I asked, "Are there other animals hiding in the trees?"

Granny said, "Yes. Lots of bats hibernate in trees. On warm nights they fly across the forest, chasing insects and pulling spiders from webs.

But even their food rests in winter. So bats snuggle up in a hollow trunk or cave, and snooze through the frosty weather."

I said, "Where do all the insects go?"

Granny told me, "Some are
sleeping right under your feet!

The ground is frozen hard.
But down below, there are stag
beetles waiting to come out.

The queen bumblebee
sleeps in a tiny tunnel.

Some moths and butterflies hide
underground, often wrapped up,
waiting for spring.

Mother earwigs look after their
eggs until they hatch when
spring comes."

We were coming to the pond. So I asked,
"What about in the water?"

Granny said, "There's ice on top
but pond life waits below.

Before it froze, frogs dived down deep
into slimy mud. Now they are still and
breathing so slowly, they seem dead!
But when the water warms in the spring,
we'll hear them croaking again."

I said, "So all sorts of animals are
having a winter sleep!"

"That's right!" Granny Sylvie told me. "Some even make a special home for winter. A bear builds a den, deep in the woods, perhaps in a cave, an old tree trunk or hidden hollow.

Mummy bear slows right down and rests there with her cubs, curled up tight on a bed she's made from soft moss, twigs and leaves."

Granny Sylvie was still telling me about
the animals in winter when I was in bed.

"You see," she told me. "There's plenty
of life tucked up, hiding in the cold."

I nodded. I could feel the cosy magic
of the dark night outside.

And even though it wasn't very late,
I closed my eyes for a winter sleep.

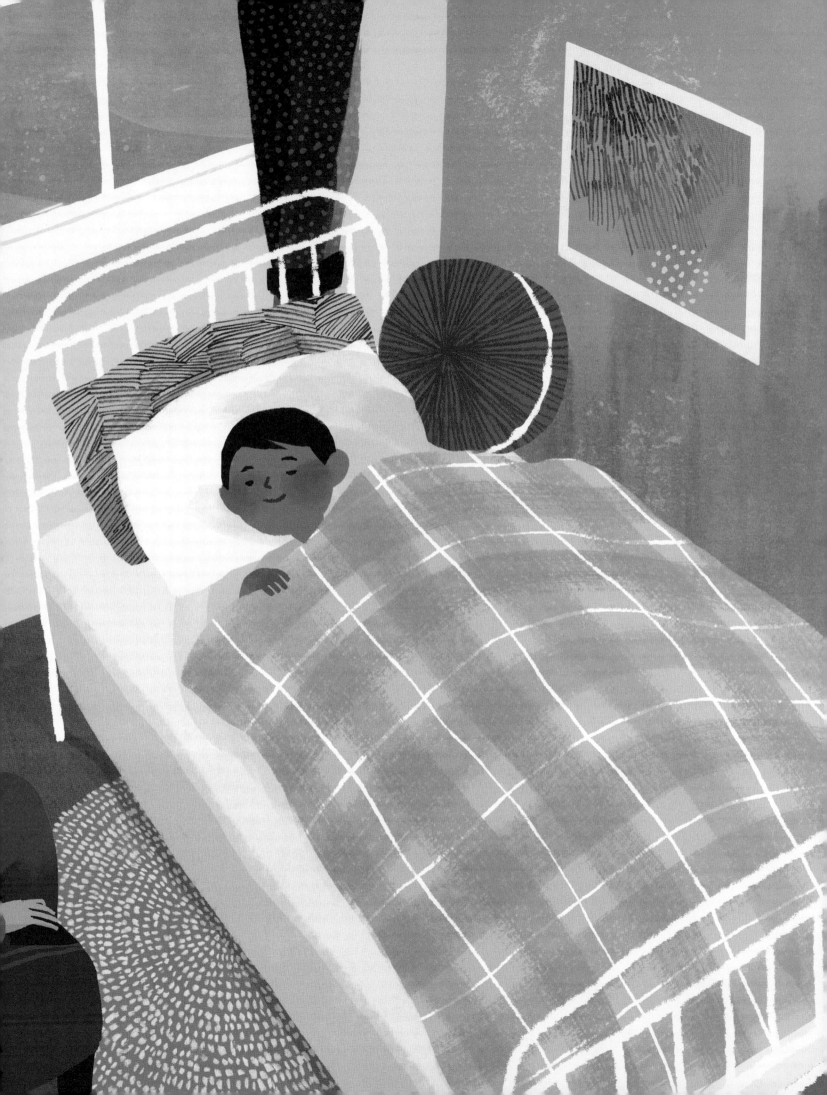

WHAT IS HIBERNATION?

Can you imagine going to bed in winter and not getting up until spring? When a snowy blanket arrives, much of the world seems sleepy. The sun feels lazy. The nights are long. Trees look undressed. Ponds freeze over. Fewer birds sing. Even the flowers are having a rest.

With plants shutting down for the colder, darker winter months, there are few flowers, fruits, nuts and leaves for animals to feed on. There are also fewer insects to eat. It is difficult for many creatures to find food and keep warm. Instead they snuggle up somewhere secret, sheltered and safe.

Hibernation is a special kind of deep sleep. It helps animals live through the coldest and hungriest times, by saving them energy. They find or make a place to hide, out of danger from hungry predators.

Mammals, reptiles, amphibians, birds and minibeasts have different kinds of winter sleep...

MAMMALS

In the winter, mammals need lots of food to keep warm and active. But where it is coldest, some hibernate instead. In autumn, they eat a lot to fatten up. Their fat protects them against the cold and gives them energy when there is no food. They become sleepier as their bodies cool down.

WOODCHUCK
When it is hibernating the woodchuck, or groundhog, might only take one breath every five minutes.

ARCTIC GROUND SQUIRREL
The Arctic ground squirrel has the coldest winter body of any hibernating mammal. It gets so cold, its brain almost freezes, and its heart only beats once per minute.

POLAR BEAR
A pregnant polar bear digs out a den in the snow. She shelters inside and hardly eats for months. When her cubs are born they will doze, snuggled up in her warm fur.

Bat

In chilly places, bats spend most of the winter hanging upside down, snoozing in their roost. They store up warm fat on their backs and bellies, to give them energy.

Deer Mouse

Deer mice cuddle up to stay warm on cold days. They also survive by making different blood which provides more energy in winter. They hide stores of snacks away from others in old, unused bird nests.

Hedgehog

A hedgehog builds a nest of leaves in winter. This is often under a shed, in an old rabbit burrow or a compost heap. As it sleeps, rolled into a tight ball, its body temperature drops from about 35 degrees Celsius to about 5 degrees Celsius.

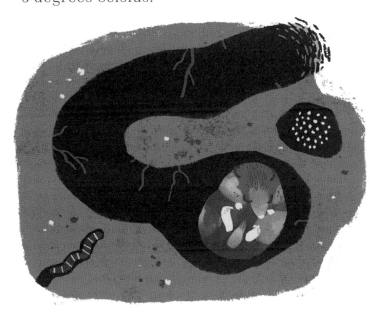

European Hamster

The wild European hamster may spend half the year hiding away deep in the earth. In her maze of underground tunnels, she is safe from most predators and sheltered from winter weather.

REPTILES, AMPHIBIANS, FISH & BIRDS

Reptiles, amphibians and fish are cold-blooded, so they can't control their body temperature. When it's freezing cold, they slow right down and most will hide themselves away. Very few birds hibernate, but some go into short rests, called torpor.

TERRAPIN
Europe's wild terrapin spends winter down at the soft, muddy bottom of a pond, lake or slow river. But it also takes a long, lazy rest in summer if it gets too hot!

TORTOISE
Some tortoises survive the cold by burying themselves in soft soil for about three months.

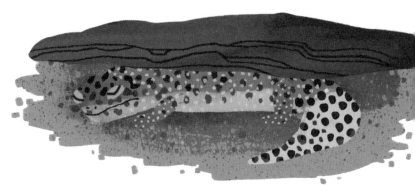

GILA MONSTER
The gila monster rests through winter and her eggs do too. She lays them in July or August, but the hatchlings don't emerge until the spring.

LEOPARD GECKO
On sunny days, geckos lay soaking up as much sunlight as they can. Then at night, they use the energy to run around feeding. But even their desert home can get cold. When the temperature drops below 10 degrees Celsius, geckos rest underground.

GRASS SNAKE

A grass snake finds a sheltered refuge underground, or in a deep pile of leaves or compost. Its winter resting place is called a hibernaculum.

SAND LIZARD

The sand lizard likes sand dunes, rocks and sandy heathland. In winter it dives down into a burrow and sometimes shares its home with other sand lizards.

WOOD FROG

In winter, wood frogs wriggle into a pile of leaves or under a log. Their heart stops, their breathing stops and they freeze almost solid.

POORWILL

Unusually for a bird, the poorwill hibernates. It retreats under rocks or logs for about 100 days.

PERCH

Perch, and some other fish, become much less active in winter. Their bodies slow down and they eat less.

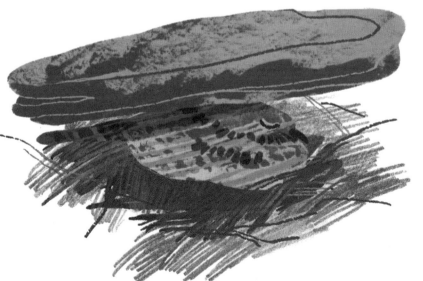

MINIBEASTS

Minibeasts have a winter sleep called diapause. Many insects, spiders, slugs and other tiny creatures live for less than one whole year, but they find ways to make sure they get through the cold. Their babies may spend time as an egg, as a sleepy larva, safely inside a cocoon, or resting. Diapause can happen for other reasons too, such as during very hot or dry times.

ARCTIC WOOLLY BEAR

The Arctic woolly bear lives in the chilliest place on Earth. Every year it wakes up for just one month. It sleeps for all the rest of its 15-year-long life.

EVEREST JUMPING SPIDER

The Everest jumping spider lives in probably the highest animal home in the world – 6,700 metres up on Mount Everest. To survive the coldest times, it needs a special liquid in its body to stop it freezing.

THE TOBACCO HORNWORM

The tobacco hornworm grows into a hawkmoth. Sunlight works like a clock for this little creature. So when the days get shorter, it wriggles down into the ground and rests.

SHORT-HORNED GRASSHOPPER

The short-horned grasshopper lays 100 tiny eggs in a burrow. She covers them in a sticky foam. This dries into a pod that protects the eggs through the winter.

KNOTGRASS MOTH

The knotgrass moth gets through winter in a cocoon disguised with leaves, grass and twigs.

GALL WASP

Oak trees often have strange wooden galls on their branches. Inside each one is the larva of a little wasp. The mum lays an egg that makes the tree grow a small house around her baby, giving it food and a safe home for winter.

WOOD ANT

Wood ants make a giant city on the forest floor, with hidden chambers underground. In winter, they get sluggish and close the doors to keep out the whooshing wind.

LADYBIRD

Adult ladybirds find shelter from the cold behind bark, under leaves or in a dry building, often in groups.

CADDISFLY

A caddisfly larva builds a tube made of silk with twigs and grit. It hides inside it all winter long at the bottom of a pond or stream.

EARTHWORM

For the winter, some earthworms burrow down and curl up in an oval-shaped chamber, deep in the soil.

HOW YOU CAN HELP

- Leave out fresh water and feeders to help birds in the cold weather.

- Create some safe winter cover for mammals. This can be done by putting up a bat box, building a log pile, or making a compost heap or wild scrubby area.

- Provide safe resting places for reptiles in compost, leaf piles, logs and rocks.

- Plant lots of flowers so there's plenty of food for minibeasts when they wake up in spring.

- Clear your pond of fallen autumn leaves so the water stays healthy for pond life during winter.

FIND OUT MORE

Amphibian and Reptile Conservation Trust: www.arc-trust.org

People's Trust for Endangered Species: www.ptes.org

Bat Conservation International: www.batcon.org

BirdLife International: www.birdlife.org

Buglife: www.buglife.org.uk